ARTHUR

AND THE

YETI

Johanne Mercier
Daniel Hahn
Clare Elsom

PHOENIX YARD BOOKS

More stories with Arthur

CONTENTS

For Michael B., who travelled the world without seeing the Yeti

JM

For Adriana

DH

For Michael

CE

Chapter 1
Mrs Potter

I'm Arthur and I'm seven, and last Saturday, at my grandparents' house in the country, we all got a bit of a fright. It all started when Mrs Potter, the lady who lives next door, rushed in.

"Oh, my dear friends," she wailed. "It's just so dreadful! It's horrible!"

"Calm down, Alison! Calm down!" Grandma said over and over again.

"If you only knew what happened last night…"

"Do tell us," said Grandad.

"At first, I heard strange noises coming from my garden. It was like there was someone scratching."

"Someone was scratching?" I asked.

"Arthur, go and play upstairs for a bit," said Grandma.

But I really, really wanted to know who had been scratching in Mrs Potter's garden, so I stayed.

"Without thinking of the danger, I bravely put my slippers on and went out with my pocket torch," Mrs Potter went on. "And guess what I saw…"

"A big grizzly bear!" said Grandad, giving me a wink.

"Was it a burglar?" asked Grandma.

"No! Two black eyes staring at me!"

"Good heavens, Alison!" cried Grandma, putting a hand to her heart. "What was it?"

"I don't know," Mrs Potter replied. "The creature ran off through my hedge towards Picket Lake."

Grandad rolled his eyes, muttering that he was sure the old lady had seen a fox prowling about. But Mrs Potter got a little bit annoyed.

"I know a fox when I see one, Geoffrey. And I can tell you that this wasn't a fox, or a cat, or a sheep. It was big, fat, grey and hairy, and it didn't smell of roses! One might have thought it was a…"

Mrs Potter stopped.

She looked a little embarrassed.

"A…?" asked Grandma.

"You won't make fun of me?"

"Absolutely not!" Grandma said.

"Geoffrey, you're not going to laugh at me either?"

"No, no," said Grandad.

"One might have thought it was some kind of monster."

Grandad burst out laughing. As for me, I ran over to the window to see if the kind-of monster was still there.

"Arthur, you're not going outside!" said Grandma, picking up the telephone.

"What are you doing?" Grandad asked her.

"I'm phoning Eugene! I want to know what he makes of all this."

"Does Cousin Eugene know about monsters?" I asked.

Grandma answered me very seriously.

"He's been a proper student, has Cousin Eugene. When you're a proper student, you get to know about things, Arthur dear."

Chapter 2
SOS Eugene

Grandma spent a long time on the phone talking to Cousin Eugene. When she hung up, her face was quite pale. Eugene hadn't reassured her at all.

"What did he say?" I asked.

"Eugene advised us to close all the windows, draw the blinds, bolt the doors and stay inside," said Grandma.

"He's overreacting," said Grandad.

"You can't be too careful with monsters," said Mrs Potter.

Fortunately, Cousin Eugene arrived just a few minutes after speaking to Grandma. He'd brought a pile of books with him, as well as a sleeping bag, a pair of binoculars, a slingshot, a big net, a penknife and some cereal bars. He looked extremely nervous.

"Good of you to come so quickly, Eugene," said Grandma, as she opened the door.

"Every minute counts in an emergency," replied Cousin Eugene, settling himself quickly at the table.

He opened his books. He leafed through them. Then he asked Mrs Potter a whole heap of questions. He wanted to know how big the monster was, what colour its fur was, if it had claws... every detail.

But Mrs Potter just kept repeating that she hadn't had the time to get a proper look; that the monster had run off too quickly; that it was very dark; and that, anyway, she hadn't even had her glasses on. Eugene looked very disappointed.

"Oh well," said Cousin Eugene, closing his books, "I'll just have to pay a visit to the scene."

"It's much too dangerous, Eugene!" cried Grandma.

"I have no choice. I have to collect evidence."

"But I've told you… I saw it!" Mrs Potter practically shouted.

"That's not enough," replied Eugene.

"Just look at poor Mrs Potter. Look how she's trembling, Eugene," Grandma went on. "Isn't that proof enough?"

Cousin Eugene took a deep breath, he gathered up his equipment, and just before leaving, he said, very seriously:

"If I'm not back in an hour, telephone for help."

Chapter 3
A Valuable Clue

I really wanted to go with Cousin Eugene to search for clues in Mrs Potter's garden, but Grandma thought it would be more sensible to play cards with Grandad and Mrs Potter than to go for a stroll outside with the monster.

We'd already played at least seven rounds of cards when Cousin Eugene came back. Grandma hugged him tightly, and I asked:

"So, did you see the monster?"

"I… I think it's about time we started

warning people," replied Eugene, his voice trembling.

Everything went quiet in the house.

"I have here a very important piece of evidence. Come and look."

We all approached Cousin Eugene, who was holding the precious clue. He opened his hand.

"Hair!" announced Eugene.

"Hair?" asked Mrs Potter, crinkling up her nose.

"I'm afraid so, Mrs Potter."

"Hair? Hair? Hair from what?" asked Grandad.

"Touch it."

We all touched the hair.

"Do you notice anything?" We all said, no, we didn't.

"Observe the unusual texture of this

hair; like a mixture of wool, horsehair and angora. It's very odd, isn't it?"

Nobody said a thing.

"There aren't any mammals, anywhere in the whole county, with a coat this shade of grey," declared Cousin Eugene. "If I add this proof to the testimony of Mrs Potter, and to the devastation the creature caused in the hedge, I can confirm, without a shadow of a doubt, that we are in the presence of a…"

"A…?"

"A yeti, Arthur!"

At that precise moment there was a huge CRASH just behind us! I thought it was the yeti arriving, but it was only our neighbour, Mrs Potter, who had fainted.

Chapter 4
Panic at Picket Lake

I was starting to get a bit nervous about all this monster business, but Grandad was quick to reassure me. He explained that yetis lived very far away, in the snowy mountains of Tibet; that there was no way one of them could have got here; and that, anyway, a yeti would have no reason to want to come for a stroll around Picket Lake.

Cousin Eugene didn't agree.

"The melting of the glaciers probably means that the yeti had to get away," said Cousin Eugene. "He's been drifting across the seas till he got here."

"Well, one thing's for sure. I'm not leaving this house till it's gone back to Tibet," announced Mrs Potter.

"We'll have to warn people," said Cousin Eugene. "We can't wait till the yeti claims its second victim."

"And might we know who the first victim was?" asked Grandad.

"That would be ME! I'M the first victim!" cried Mrs Potter. "See! I'm still shaking."

"Grandad! Look outside!"

Through the window I could see loads of people heading towards Picket Lake. They were all carrying cameras.

"How could they have known?" asked Grandad.

"I… Well, I… I warned a lady to look out for the yeti just now," admitted Cousin Eugene, slightly embarrassed.

Grandad and I decided to go and see what was happening outside.

"Hey, just hang on a minute, you two!" growled Grandma, as she saw us leaving. "You aren't planning to go off and throw yourselves right into the yeti's mouth, I hope?"

Grandad told her not to worry, that he knew what to do if we came across the yeti. All you had to do was look it straight in the eyes like you did with bears, and tickle its belly like you did with crocodiles. Grandma didn't seem reassured, but she let us go out.

"You here for the yeti?" asked a man with a pair of binoculars, when he saw us approaching the lake. "By my calculations, he'll be surfacing for breath a few minutes from now."

"How does he stay underwater?" I asked.

"Yetis are just like whales, young man, only hairier."

"Er ... no," said Grandad.

"Oh, but they are. They really are very hairy."

Grandad and I walked on.

"And to think that only yesterday I was swimming in this lake," said Mrs Harvey, when she saw my grandfather.

"I can tell you now, I'm putting my house up for sale!" cried Mrs Hudson. "There's no way I'm going to live in a village infested with yetis!"

Then a fat man with a cigar walked over, saying:

"I'll buy it! I'll buy your house!"

Then he added, with a smile, "I'll open a café with a view over the lake!

"The *Yeti Café*, that's it! I'll serve yeti burgers and yeti butties! Yes, what a brilliant idea I've had!"

Then a lady appeared, quite excited, waving a photo. She said she had proof that her uncle had spotted the yeti last month.

All you could see in the photo was the shadow of something very blurry, but everyone said, "Oh, how frightful!" when they saw it.

Then the security men got out of their big vans and asked us to leave. They explained that they had to find the monster's footprints and carry out some tests.

And when nobody moved, they added:

"You know, yetis don't just eat frogs and daffodils…"

Everyone was terrified that the yeti might be munching on them at any moment. But even though they were all trembling with fear, it wasn't till the end of the afternoon that they started to leave.

"Not a lot of yetis around here," sighed one disappointed man.

"Good thing no one made us pay to see this," added his wife.

And everyone left: the security men,
Mrs Harvey, Mrs Hudson, the lady with
the photo, the man with the cigar, even the
one with the binoculars, who was still
repeating over and over:

"According to my calculations, the
yeti should be surfacing for breath any
minute now."

The only people left on the bank of the

lake were me, my grandfather, and a big hairy dog, who looked lost. As the dog seemed friendly, I asked Grandad if I could keep him.

"I don't think your grandmother would be very happy to be visited by a huge dog," answered Grandad, stroking the animal's head.

Then he added: "But we can always give

it a try!"

So all three of us went back to the house.

Chapter 5
Proof!

When we arrived, Grandma, Mrs Potter and Cousin Eugene were in the kitchen, having tea with frosted biscuits. They weren't talking about the yeti any more. They were quite calm, till Grandma saw us.

"Oh, you can't be serious! Now what have you brought me? Arthur, you put that dog outside at once!"

"He's all alone, Grandma. If we leave him outside, the yeti will eat him alive!"

"Arthur, we've already got your duck here. That's more than enough!"

"But a duck isn't the same. And anyway, the dog can warn us if the yeti comes near the house."

"That's certainly true," added Cousin Eugene. "It's always wise to equip oneself with a canine when there's a yeti around."

"Just look at all the hair this canine of yours has already started leaving on my rug!" grumbled Grandma.

Grandad rushed off to fetch the dustpan and brush.

"Hang on! Hang on a minute," said Grandad as he gathered up the hair. "Eugene, would you come over here a moment?"

Cousin Eugene got up. Grandma, Mrs Potter and I came over, too.

"These are dog hairs!" announced Grandad.

"Of course they are dog hairs," said Grandma. "What did you think they'd be?"

"Touch them!" said Grandad.

We touched them.

And…

They were exactly the same as the hairs from the yeti!

ARTHUR

Johanne Mercier

It all started when this lady called Johanne thought about me in her head. Grandma said Johanne had written fifty-eight stories for children, and that one of her stories was made into a film. Grandma also said Johanne understands children because she used to be a teacher. But now she writes all day.

I think it must be really fun to write stories all day. When I grow up, I want to write stories like Johanne Mercier, and I also want to be a pilot. Grandad says there's nothing to stop me doing both, but I think that writing stories and flying a plane at the same time is not a good idea.

Daniel Hahn

Daniel Hahn translated the stories. He took my French words, and wrote them in English. He said it was quite a difficult job, but Cousin Eugene said he could have done it much better, only he was busy that day. So we got Daniel to do it, as he's translated loads and loads of books before. He also said he wrote the words for a book called *Happiness is a Watermelon on your Head*, but everyone else said that book was just plain silly.

Daniel is almost as clever as Cousin Eugene and he lives in England, in a house by the sea, with a lot of books.

Clare Elsom

I was so happy when we met Clare Elsom. She got out her pencils and pens and scribbled until the scribbles looked just like me! Grandma and Grandad said the resemblance was uncanny.

Clare has so many pencils and pens – at least twenty of them – and she spends all day drawing in lots of different books. I'm not sure that you are allowed to draw in books, but she seems to get away with it.

I like Clare because she likes egg on toast and exploring new places, and drawing me. But I think she wants my pet duck, so I will have to keep an eye on her.

More escapades with
Arthur coming soon

Arthur and the Witch
Arthur and the Ice Rink

Also available

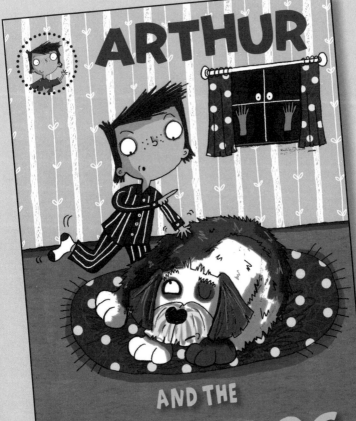

ARTHUR

AND THE
GUARD DOG

JOHANNE MERCIER

Arthur and the Yeti
ISBN: 978-1-907912-18-4

First published in French in 2008 under the title *Arthur et le yéti du lac Pichette*
by Dominique et compagnie, a division of Les Editions Heritage, Saint-Lambert,
Canada. This edition published in the UK by Phoenix Yard Books Ltd, 2013.

Phoenix Yard Books
Phoenix Yard
65 King's Cross Road
London
WC1X 9LW
www.phoenixyardbooks.com

Text copyright © Johanne Mercier, 2008
English translation copyright © Daniel Hahn, 2013
Illustrations copyright © Clare Elsom, 2013

1 3 5 7 9 10 8 6 4 2
A CIP catalogue record for this book is available from the British Library
Printed in China